Walking with Dinosaurs: Patchi's Big Adventure

BBC, BBC Earth and Walking with Dinosaurs are trademarks of the British Broadcasting Corporation and are used under license.

Walking with Dinosaurs logo © BBC 2012

BBC logo © BBC 1996

© 2013 BBC Earth MD (WWD) Limited, Evergreen MD LLC and Reliance Prodco LLC

Library of Congress catalog card number: 2013934069

ISBN 978-0-06-223275-5

Typography by Rick Farley

13 14 15 16 17 LP/PO/WOR 10 9 8 7 6 5 4 3 2 1

❖

First Edition

WALKING WITH DINOSAURS THE 3D MOVIE

Patchi's Big Adventure

Adapted by J. E. Bright

HARPER FESTIVAL
An Imprint of HarperCollins*Publishers*

Patchi is a plant-eating Pachyrhinosaurus. He's the smallest of all the hatchlings, born only four weeks ago.

All Patchi's brothers and sisters are bigger and stronger than he is. But Patchi is determined to get his fair share of food! He sees some on the far edge of the nest and heads that way.

A hungry Troodon spots the hatchlings eating. A few of the Pachyrhinosaurus see the Troodon and start to worry, but Patchi doesn't notice and keeps eating.

The Troodon snatches Patchi out of the nest. He takes off with Patchi wriggling and squealing in his jaws.

The Troodon darts between trees and around nests, trying to find a way out. He has to escape the Pachyrhinosaurus nesting grounds before he can rest. Patchi kicks and squirms, but he can't get free.

Patchi's mother bellows at the Troodon to release her baby.

Spinning around, the Troodon avoids Patchi's mom. He carries Patchi through the maze of pathways between nests, trying to escape.

But suddenly, another Pachyrhinosaurus is after him. It's Patchi's father, Bulldust!

Bulldust blocks the Troodon's path, and the Troodon suddenly loses his grip on the young Pachyrhinosaurus. Patchi tumbles through the air.

Patchi lands far from the Pachyrhinosaurus nests,
in a patch of ferns. He shakes his head. The Troodon's
teeth left a hole in his frill!

Patchi peeks out from under the
ferns as an enormous foot slams
down next to him. He follows the adult
dinosaur, thinking it's his mother!

Patchi can't keep up with the adult dinosaur, though. He's tired, lost, and filthy.
He spots a shiny dragonfly and stops to stare at its shimmering colors. When it zips off, Patchi chases the dragonfly, snapping at it.

Suddenly, an Alphadon snatches the dragonfly out of the air and swallows it in one gulp!

The Alphadon spots Patchi. He gets close enough to sniff the young Pachyrhinosaurus, then wrinkles up his nose and races away. Patchi chases after him.

Patchi follows the Alphadon along the
worn trail, but loses him around a curve. He
finds an enormous Ankylosaurus instead!
The Ankylosaurus is a plant eater, too.
But his armored, scaly head scares Patchi.

Patchi runs as fast as he can, charging through the darkest part of the woods. He heads for a circle of light in the distance.

Bursting out of the trees, Patchi sees a spectacular view. Below is a deep valley with a blue lagoon surrounded by hundreds of dinosaurs. Patchi watches a group of pterosaurs fly to the far shore.

He sees another group of dinosaurs much closer to him. Some Hesperonychus have surrounded the Alphadon Patchi saw in the woods. It is pretending to be dead. When the Hesperonychus see Patchi, the Alphadon jumps up and flees!

The Hesperonychus chase Patchi back into the forest, but before they can catch him, a giant mouth scoops him high into the air.

It's Patchi's mother!

She scares away the nasty Hesperonychus.

Patchi's mother carries him back to the hatching grounds and nuzzles him into her nest with his brothers and sisters. Patchi is glad to be back home and safe!